For Thea, both loving and kind —A.W.P.

Especially for Sam! —D.W.

Farrar Straus Giroux Books for Young Readers
An imprint of Macmillan Publishing Group, LLC
120 Broadway, New York, NY 10271
mackids.com

Our books may be purchased in bulk for promotional, educational, or business use.
Please contact your local bookseller or the Macmillan Corporate and Premium Sales Department at (800) 221-7945 ext. 5442
or by email at MacmillanSpecialMarkets@macmillan.com.

Library of Congress Cataloging-in-Publication Data
Names: Paul, Ann Whitford, author. | Walker, David, 1965– illustrator.
Title: If animals tried to be kind / Ann Whitford Paul ; pictures by David Walker.
Description: First edition. | New York: Farrar Straus Giroux, 2021. | Audience: Ages 2–6. | Audience: Grades K–1. | Summary:
Explores how different members of the animal kingdom might show kindness to one another.
Identifiers: LCCN 2020010527 | ISBN 9780374313425 (hardcover)
Subjects: CYAC: Stories in rhyme. | Kindness—Fiction. | Animals—Habits and behavior—Fiction.
Classification: LCC PZ8.3.P273645 Ifm 2021 | DDC [E]—dc23
LC record available at https://lccn.loc.gov/2020010527

First edition, 2021
Book design by Aram Kim
Color separations by Bright Arts (H.K.) Ltd.
Printed in China by Toppan Leefung Printing Ltd., Dongguan City, Guangdong Province

ISBN 978-0-374-31342-5 (hardcover)
1 3 5 7 9 10 8 6 4 2

If Animals Tried to Be Kind

Ann Whitford Paul
Pictures by David Walker

Farrar Straus Giroux
New York

If animals tried to be kind like we do,

Porcupine would choose two quill needles to knit
a scarf for Giraffe, long enough to fit.

Gator would offer Raccoon a ride
on his scaly canoe to the swamp's other side.

Hyena would laugh, mocking Wildebeest,

until Lion **roooooaaaaared**—
then the teasing would cease.

Pig would spy Sheep, sad, alone by a rock,

and start up a lively **oink**-and-**baa** talk.

If animals tried to be kind like we do,
Porcupine would keep knitting—
knitty-knit-knit—
needing more rows
for Giraffe's scarf to fit.

Seal would make room on her icy floe boat
so she and Penguin could share a fun float.

Bear would surprise his best buddy Snake
with a tasty, *sweet yum-yum* honey cake.

When old Owl couldn't see very well anymore,
Hawk would pitch in with her food-hunting chore.

If animals tried to be kind like we do,
Porcupine's needles would **knitty-knit-knit**,
but Giraffe's scarf?

Still not long enough to fit.

Gently Stork would lift Lizard, *sooo-ooar* her up high,

so one time, at least, she'd be close to the sky.

Squirrel would see Dog **dig-diggity-dig** and help in his bone search, *DIG-dig-dig-DIG.*

Cat would let Mouse snuggle next to her fur
and hush Mouse to sleep with her lullaby *purrrrrrr*.

If animals tried to be kind like we do,
when Porcupine had no more yarn to knit,

she'd bind off the scarf
and Bird would **wrap-wrappity** it...

round and
round, *round,*
round,
round,
round—

a perfect fit!

Then Giraffe would hum thanks and, pleased as can be,

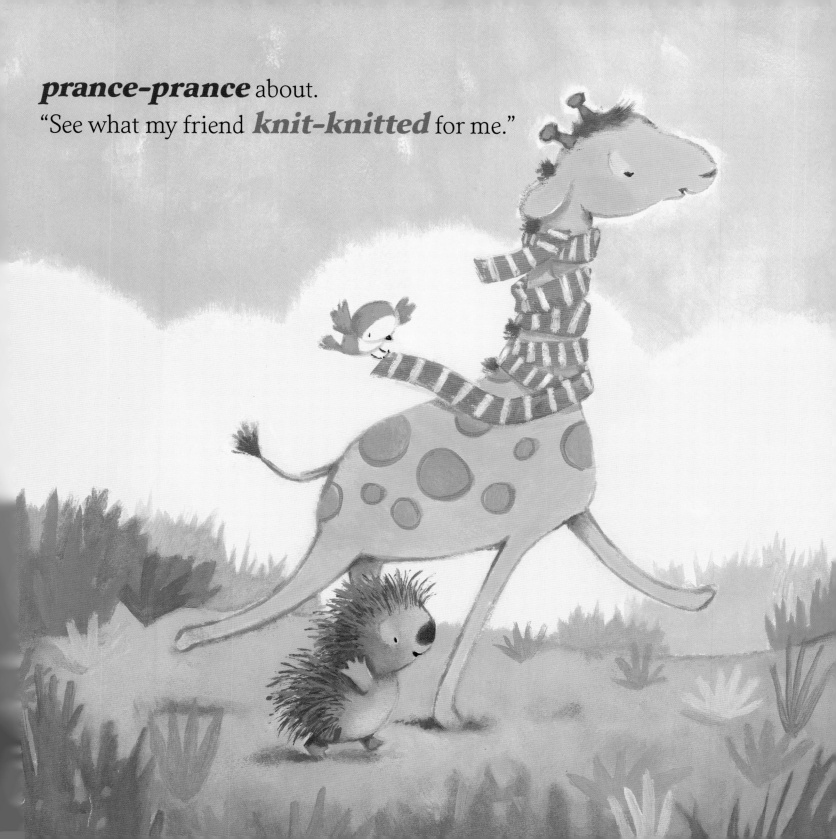

prance-prance about.
"See what my friend **knit-knitted** for me."